S0-BEZ-047

KIDS CAN'T STOP READING
THE *CHOOSE YOUR*
OWN ADVENTURE® STORIES!

"I like *Choose Your Own Adventure*®
books because they're full of surprises.
I can't wait to read more."
—Cary Romanos, age 12

"Makes you think thoroughly before
making a decision."
—Hassan Stevenson, age 11

"I have read five different stories in
one night and that's a record for me.
The different endings are fun."
—Timmy Sullivan, age 9

"It's great fun! I like the idea of
making my own decisions."
—Anthony Ziccardi, age 11

AND TEACHERS
LIKE THIS SERIES, TOO!

"We have read and reread,
wore thin, loved, loaned, bought for others,
and donated to school libraries, the
Choose Your Own Adventure® books."

CHOOSE YOUR OWN ADVENTURE®—
AND MAKE READING MORE FUN!

Bantam Books in the Choose Your Own Adventure® Series
Ask your bookseller for the books you have missed

Choose Your Own Adventure® Series for young readers

KINGSWAY REGIONAL HIGH SCHOOL
LIBRARY
WOOLWICH TOWNSHIP
SWEDESBORO, NEW JERSEY 08085

JOURNEY UNDER THE SEA

R. A. MONTGOMERY

ILLUSTRATED BY PAUL GRANGER

BANTAM BOOKS

TORONTO • NEW YORK • LONDON • SYDNEY • AUCKLAND

RL 5, IL age 10 and up

JOURNEY UNDER THE SEA

A Bantam Book
PRINTING HISTORY
Originally published by Vermont Crossroads Press, 1977

Bantam edition / July 1979

2nd printing . . . December 1979	8th printing . . December 1981
3rd printing . . . . May 1980	9th printing . . . . June 1982
4th printing . . . . July 1980	10th printing . . . . . August 1982
5th printing . . . September 1980	11th printing . . . . . August 1982
6th printing . . . . March 1981	12th printing . . November 1982
7th printing . . . . July 1981	13th printing . . December 1983

14th printing . . September 1984

CHOOSE YOUR OWN ADVENTURE is a
registered trademark of Bantam Books, Inc.,
Registered in U.S. Patent and Trademark Office and elsewhere.

Original conception of Edward Packard

Illustrations by Paul Granger

All rights reserved.
Copyright © 1977 by Raymond A. Montgomery, Jr.
Illustrations copyright © 1979 by Bantam Books, Inc.
This book may not be reproduced in whole or in part, by
mimeograph or any other means, without permission.
For information address: Writers House, Inc.,
21 West 26th Street, New York, New York 10010.

ISBN 0-553-23229-0

Published simultaneously in the United States and Canada

Bantam Books are published by Bantam Books, Inc. Its trademark, consisting of the words "Bantam Books" and the por-
trayal of a rooster is Registered in U.S. Patent and Trademark
Office and in other countries. Marca Registrada. Bantam
Books, Inc., 666 Fifth Avenue, New York, New York 10103.

PRINTED IN THE UNITED STATES OF AMERICA

O   23 22 21 20 19 18 17 16

For My Friends
Ramsey and Anson

WARNING! ! ! !

Do not read this book straight through from beginning to end! These pages contain many different adventures you can go on as you journey under the sea. From time to time as you read along, you will be asked to make a choice. Your choice may lead to success or disaster!

The adventures you take are a result of your choice. *You* are responsible because *you* choose! After you make your choice follow the instructions to see what happens to you next.

Remember—you cannot go back! Think carefully before you make a move! One mistake can be your last . . . or it *may* lead you to fame and fortune!

You are an underwater explorer. You are leaving to explore the deepest oceans. You must find the lost city of Atlantis. This is your most challenging assignment.

It is morning and the sun pushes up on the horizon. The sea is calm. You climb into the narrow pilot's compartment of the underwater vessel *Seeker* with your special gear. The crew of the research vessel *Maray* screws down the hatch clamps. Now begins the plunge into the depths of the ocean. The *Seeker* crew begins lowering by a strong, but thin cable. Within minutes, you are so deep in the ocean that little light filters down to you. The silence is eerie as the *Seeker* slips deeper and deeper. You peer out the thick glass porthole and see fish drifting past, sometimes stopping to look at you—an intruder from another world.

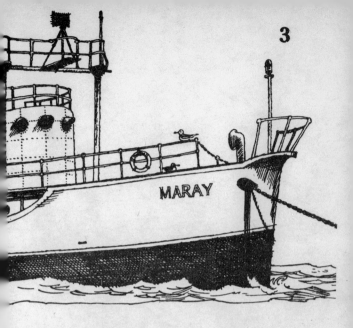

Now the cable attaching you to *Maray* is extended almost to its limit. You have come to rest on a ledge near the canyon in the ocean floor that supposedly leads to the lost city of Atlantis.

You have a special sea suit that will protect you from the intense pressure of the deep if you choose to walk about on the sea bottom. You can cut loose from the cable if you wish because the *Seeker* is self-propelled. You are now in another world.

If you decide to explore the ledge where the Seeker has come to rest, turn to page 6.

If you decide to cut loose from the Maray and dive with the Seeker into the canyon in the ocean floor, turn to page 5.

You radio a status report to the *Maray* and tell them that you are going to cast off from the line and descend under your own power. Your plan is approved and you cast off your line. Now you are on your own. The *Seeker* slips noiselessly into the undersea canyon.

As you drop into the canyon, you turn on the *Seeker's* powerful searchlight. Straight ahead is a dark wall covered with a strange type of barnacle growth. To the left (port) side you see what appears to be a grotto. The entrance is perfectly round, as if it had been cut by human hands.

Lantern fish give off a pale, greenish light. To the right (starboard) side of the *Seeker* you see bubbles rising steadily from the floor of the canyon.

If you decide to investigate the bubbles, turn to page 8.

If you decide to investigate the grotto with the round entrance, turn to page 9.

Your sea suit will protect you from the intense pressures of the deep. It is a tight fit and takes you some time to put it on. Finally you slip from the airlock of the *Seeker* and stand on the ocean floor. It is a strange and marvelous world where your every move is slowed down. You begin to explore with your special hand-held searchlight. You examine the ledge by the canyon.

Suddenly, a school of bright yellow angel fish dart by, almost brushing you. What made them move so fast? Are they being chased?

Then you see it. The *Seeker* is in the grips of a huge sea monster. It is similar to a squid, but it is enormous. The *Seeker* is just a toy in its long, powerful tentacles. You seek shelter behind a rock formation. You know the spear gun you carry will be useless against this monster. It looks as though it will destroy the *Seeker*. Fish of all sizes huddle with you in an attempt to escape the monster.

If you stay hidden close to the Seeker, turn to page 10.

If you try to escape in the hope that rescuers will see you, turn to page 12.

Carefully, you maneuver the *Seeker* between the walls of the canyon.

On the floor of the canyon, you discover a large round hole out of which flow the large bubbles. The *Seeker* is equipped with scientific equipment to analyze the bubbles. It also has sonar equipment that can measure the depth of any hole.

*If you decide to analyze the bubbles,
turn to page 11*

*If you decide to take sonar readings
turn to page 15*

You pilot the *Seeker* through the rounded entrance to the grotto. Once inside, your searchlight picks up what appear to be docks and piers along the grotto walls. The *Seeker's* searchlight is not very powerful. However, you do have a special laser light which would light up the grotto like daylight. Unfortunately, the laser light can only be used twice for very short periods before it must be recharged aboard the *Maray*, now more than 2,000 feet above you on the surface.

If you decide to use the laser light, turn to page 16.

If you decide to cruise further into the grotto, turn to page 14.

The giant squid tosses and turns the *Seeker*, but finally the creature grows tired of its new game and jets off with an enormous squirt of water. You now are free to leave your hiding place and examine the *Seeker* for damage.

To your dismay, the airlock entrance has been jammed shut. You are locked out of the *Seeker*. The crew of the *Maray*, however, suspected trouble when you did not respond to a routine radio check and they are now lowering an escape platform to you. Once on the platform, you radio them to start the slow pull to the surface. To avoid the bends—rapid expansion of nitrogen bubbles in your blood—they will have to bring you up very slowly.

Just as the platform begins to move, the giant squid suddenly returns as if from nowhere. It is headed directly at you.

If you decide to fight the squid with your spear gun, hoping to scare it off, turn to page 17.

If you decide to signal Maray to pull you up at top speed, knowing you will get the bends, turn to page 18.

You squeeze into your sea suit and, outside the *Seeker,* you use special equipment to analyze the bubbles. As you work, you clumsily knock against the valve that dumps the compressed air necessary to make the *Seeker* rise to the surface. There is nothing to be done about it; so you continue to analyze the bubbles. They contain a high percentage of oxygen and no poisonous gases. Perhaps they are coming from some area below the sea where human-type beings can live and breathe. Perhaps they are coming from Atlantis.

You wonder whether you should try the *Seeker's* drilling arm to enlarge the source of the bubbles so you can explore it with the *Seeker.* But you are also very worried about the *Seeker's* loss of rising capability. You might also be able to trap the bubbles and use them to raise the *Seeker.*

If you try to collect the bubbles coming from the hole to fill the tanks of the Seeker, *turn to page 24.*

If you decide to drill, turn to page 22.

Moving cautiously, you climb up the sides of the canyon hoping to reach the ocean floor. You leave the *Seeker* in the grips of the giant squid. Your plan is to signal for help with a dye marker that will float to the surface and make a bright yellow patch in the water. The crewmen above have been instructed to watch for such emergency signals. They will send help.

Once you reach the ledge above the canyon and feel slightly safer, you see the most feared of all sea creatures—a huge shark. It begins to circle towards you and you know that you are its target. You wonder whether you should fire your emergency propulsion charge that will send you rapidly to the surface. The shark is fast; he might catch you anyway. You also know that you will get the bends from the rapid rise to the surface.

If you decide to fire the special propulsion charge to get to the surface, turn to page 21.

If you decide to wait quietly hoping that the shark will go away turn to page 19.

EKER

You cruise silently into the grotto. Its roof seems to slope upward and you follow the slope. The depth finder shows that you are rising quite rapidly. Perhaps you will reach the surface and open air. Then the roof of the grotto stops sloping upward. Before you is a perfectly round metallic hatch made of a metal that you have never seen before. With the mechanical arm of the *Seeker* you try to open the hatch. It will not open. You begin to send radio signals at the door hoping to make contact on the other side.

If you decide to blow the hatch open with an explosive charge, turn to page 26.

If you decide to continue transmitting radio communications through the hatch, turn to page 28.

You maneuver the *Seeker* next to the hole and begin to take sonar readings to determine the depth of the hole. To your amazement, the sonar readings indicate that the hole is extraordinarily deep—it might reach the center of the earth!

What lies down there? Where are the bubbles coming from? Is Atlantis beneath you?

Then you notice a disturbing reading on your instruments; a mild earthquake has occurred. The *Seeker* is not damaged, but the earthquake could set up a tsunami wave on the surface causing the *Maray* to leave for safer areas. It might be dangerous not to get back to the surface and leave with the *Maray*. On the other hand, you are perhaps on the verge of one of the world's greatest discoveries.

*If you decide to descend into the hole,
turn to page 23.*

*If you decide to return to the surface,
turn to page 27.*

The beam from the laser light illuminates the entire grotto. Far back on the floor of the grotto is a submarine! Cautiously, you maneuver the *Seeker* closer. You identify it as the submarine that mysteriously disappeared in the Bermuda Triangle almost a year before. The Bermuda Triangle is more than 2000 miles away.

The submarine is apparently not damaged, but it is covered with a slimy algae. Beautiful fish swim around it as though it is their own special prize. Then you notice that the main hatch is free of algae!

*If you decide to try
to enter the submarine,
turn to page 29*

*If you decide to cruise on through
the grotto, turn to page 31*

With a rush of water, the giant squid attacks you. Two 20-foot tentacles with their pulsing suction cups reach out trying to ensnare you. You dive off the platform and rapidly fire two of your spears. They strike the squid close to its two monstrous eyes. But the squid keeps on coming.

One of the tentacles wraps around your diving helmet and ruptures the seal to your suit. You fire your last spear hoping to hit the monster in a vulnerable spot. Water is beginning to trickle into your suit. You signal the *Maray* to haul you up fast—"Emergency Hoist." You must have hit the squid. It floats away writhing and thrashing. You think you're about to black out.

You wake up on the deck of the *Maray* and are quickly rushed to the decompression chambers to ward off the effect of the bends. In a few days you are better and start to worry about diving into the abyss again.

If you decide to quit the expedition now, turn to page 32.

If you decide to go back down to the deep, turn to page 33.

18

As they begin the rapid hauling, you lose your
ability to function in the deep. You start to get dizzy,
and your arms and legs feel weak. You lose your
hold on the platform and drift in the water
exhausted. Then you see a dolphin heading toward you. You know that these marvelous
mammals sometimes help people in trouble. Will it
help you?

*If you try to get help from
the dolphin, turn to page 34*

*If you decide to carr
on alone swimming to th
surface, turn to page 37*

You wait for the shark to go away. But then you notice other sharks coming to join in the hunt. They circle you, coming closer and faster each time. It is too late. There is no escape!

The End

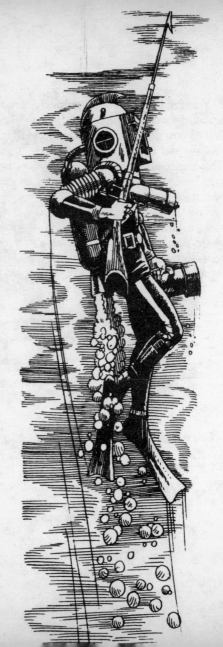

You fire the special propulsion charge and zoom upward through the water, frightening schools of fish as you go. You become dizzy and lose track of where you are. The world seems upside down. The shark is nowhere around, you hope. Then you break through to the surface floating about a half mile from the *Maray*.

The lookouts spot you in the water and quickly rescue you. Unfortunately, the rapid ascent has given you a bad case of the bends. It takes a long time to decompress. And when you are finally all right, the ship's doctor informs you that your underwater days are over. Someone else will have to find Atlantis.

The End

As you begin to drill, the stream of bubbles increases.

The stream of bubbles is strong enough now to ruffle the surface of the sea. You could try to surface now and locate the exact position of the bubble area. Then you could make plans with the scientists aboard the *Maray* about what to do next. But also, you could simply explore the hole with the *Seeker* to determine the source of the bubbles now! There is great risk in entering the hole, but it could lead to the source of the bubbles and maybe to Atlantis.

If you explore, turn to page 38.

If you try to surface, turn to page 35.

Now is the time for decision. You check all the controls of the *Seeker,* grit your teeth, and push the control column into the deep dive position. Down, down you go where no person has ever ventured. The *Seeker* is built for deep, deep dives, but you are descending rapidly mile after mile into the deep. The pressure is intense, the darkness is complete, and the depth guage indicates an incredible 15 miles. You quickly reverse the control column. Warning lights flare up on your control panel; they show that gravitational forces are now stronger than the *Seeker's* propulsion motors. You have passed the point of no return and your journey downward will continue in utter darkness until the water pressure is too great for the *Seeker.* This is the final voyage.

The End

24

You are able to capture the bubbling gases and fill the tanks of the *Seeker,* enough to allow it to rise. Slowly, the *Seeker* rises out of the canyon, scattering schools of brightly colored fish, and brushing past underwater plants that wave like palm trees in a wind. Just as you reach the ledge at the top of the canyon, you see what appears to be an old road! Rocks along its side seem to be guard rails. Could this be a path that leads to the lost city of Atlantis? You anchor the *Seeker* and prepare to investigate more closely.

Turn to page 6.

KINGSWAY REGIONAL HIGH SCHOOL
LIBRARY
WOOLWICH TOWNSHIP
SWEDESBORO, NEW JERSEY 08085

The only way to get beyond the door is to blast it away, or so you believe. The *Seeker's* laser cannon is powerful and you position the *Seeker* to fire. Pushing the fire button, you send a powerful beam at the hatch. Nothing happens. Then you advance the cannon control to full emergency force. Again you push the button and the beam dissolves the hatch instantly. A flood of sea water rushes into the giant hole, carrying you with it into an air-filled cavern beyond. The water fills the cavern with speed and explosive force. You see several people scurrying towards escape hatches. *IT IS TOO LATE!* You did the wrong thing.

The End

Deciding to return to the surface, you direct the *Seeker* cautiously back along the side of the canyon in the ocean floor. Without warning, the *Seeker* is gripped in a powerful current that sweeps it toward a grotto. Once in the grotto, the current carries you to what appears to be a large metal door. It swings open and the *Seeker* is swept inside. The door closes, the water in the grotto drains away, and you step out into a chamber that you decide must be made by human hands.

A door opens in the wall, two people dressed in simple clothes come towards you. One of them says, "Welcome to Atlantis. We have been expecting you."

What a discovery! You have found the lost continent and its civilization. The two people tell you that although citizens of Atlantis occasionally journey to the upper world, anyone who happens upon Atlantis is never permitted to leave. The Atlanteans are not cruel but fear discovery of their world.

They want you to follow them and you agree. But you have another thought. Perhaps you could blast your way out of the chamber with the *Seeker's* laser cannon.

If you decide to follow the people and join the Atlantean society, turn to page 39.

If you decide to make a dash for the Seeker and try to blast through the closed door with the laser cannon, turn to page 40.

28

The radio transmissions seem to be failing, and you grow tired of sending signals through the closed door. You are just about to give up when the door suddenly swings open revealing behind it a cavern with another door. You enter the cavern cautiously and receive a radio signal in English. It tells you that you are welcome here, but that once you enter this place, you may never return to the world above. It is up to you to decide.

If you decide to go on
and investigate what might be Atlantis,
turn to page 41

If you decide to retreat, turn to page 42

The submarine is indeed mysterious. You now have on your sea suit and you open the hatch on the conning tower and enter the sub. It is amazingly clean and in order. There are no signs of life, but there are also no signs of struggle or trouble. In the control room, you see a piece of mystifying equipment that just doesn't belong on this sub.

A voice begins telling you that, thousands of years ago, the leaders of Atlantis realized that their continent was slipping into the sea. They discovered a large underground cavern and built new forms of living quarters for their people. Later when Atlantis was deep beneath the ocean, some of their scientists discovered and perfected an operation enabling them to breathe under water.

The voice, which sounds friendly, also tells you that there are two groups in Atlantis. One group is good and the other is evil. The voice invites you to enter the world of Atlantis and gives directions and instructions to a secret passageway to the underwater city.

As you follow directions, you spy an unbelievable underwater craft with several people in it. It must be an Atlantean ship, but are the people good or evil? Do they know of the secret passageway?

If you hurry in, trying to reach the secret passageway without being seen, turn to page 43.

If you rush back to the Seeker trying to escape danger, turn to page 44.

You cruise through the grotto past the wreck of the submarine and then you spot another ship wreck. And then another. They, too, are covered with algae, but they appear undamaged. Maybe people from Atlantis capture ships in the Bermuda Triangle and bring them here. Then you see another ship, but this one is a three-masted schooner of the type used in the early 1800s. Its rigging is festooned with algae, and fish swim lazily around its mast.

Your curiosity captures you and you put on your sea suit. Leaving the *Seeker,* you move towards the old sailing ship. Suddenly a thirteen-foot long deadly poisonous sea snake strikes from behind the forward cabin and bites you in the soft flesh between the fingers of your right hand. There is no antidote to the deadly poison.

The End

With great sorrow, you decide that it is wisest to leave the expedition now. You can't risk returning to the great depths below. So, you reluctantly return to the United States.

You are invited to tell of your adventures on several major television shows. While on one such show, a special news flash announces to the world the discovery of Atlantis. You regret your decision, but you didn't really have a choice. Did you?

The End

You can't resist the adventure beneath the sea. You must go down again, and after several weeks of rest, you enter the *Seeker* and slip quickly into the deep. You bring the *Seeker* to rest by the great canyon in the ocean bottom and, wearing your special suit, you venture out into the depths. There are no signs of the giant squid and you feel safe.

Rounding a rock formation, you come upon the wreck of an ancient Greek ship. How strange to find this ship, intact, so far below the surface. What brought it here? Was it visiting Atlantis before the lost continent slipped beneath the sea?

You take pictures and make notes in your special undersea book. Maybe this ancient ship hides the secret to Atlantis.

If you go aboard the Greek ship, turn to page 45.

If you return to the surface to report your findings, turn to page 46.

The dolphin looks at you, and you even imagine that he is smiling at you. You grab one of his flippers and with a powerful switch of his body, the dolphin swims upward. In a short time, you break through to the surface. You blink in the bright sun. The *Maray* is nowhere in sight. You are lost far at sea.

The dolphin dives beneath the surface with you still clinging to him. He speeds off and within 20 minutes you are next to the *Maray*. The dolphin must have heard the *Maray's* engine noises underneath the water.

Once aboard, everyone congratulates you on your escape. You will go down again, but the thought keeps haunting you: What if your luck has run out?

If you decide to dive again the next day, turn to page 48.

If you decide to give up the expedition, turn to page 47.

You suddenly realize the stream of bubbles is powerful enough to raise the *Seeker*. You guide the *Seeker* into the bubble stream and it heads towards the surface. As you swirl upward, you begin to notice increasing amounts of brown kelp—seaweed. Near the surface, you become entangled in the seaweed. The instruments in the *Seeker* indicate that the propellers and the steering mechanisms will not work.

You put on your sea suit and go out to see what can be done. Once outside in the kelp, you realize that you can't free the *Seeker*. You start to swim for the surface but then you are soon completely stuck in the clinging seaweed. You are trapped and unable to go forward or return to the *Seeker*.

If you decide to keep struggling towards the surface, turn to page 50.

If you decide to rest quietly, gain strength, and work out a plan, turn to page 53.

The dolphin might help and might not. You decide to chance it alone. So, up you head, swimming towards the surface. The dolphin follows for some time, and then swims off. You rest for awhile about 300 feet below the surface before your final ascent.

Then a large fish—ugly, lumpy, puffed up, and covered with black and white markings swims towards you. Its bulging eyes fasten on you. It is a *big-mouthed grouper,* a fish which does not bother to bite its victims, but simply swallows them whole.

It looks as though you are its next meal.

The End

You decide to guide the *Seeker* into the new passageway to the bubble source. Suddenly the *Seeker* is swept downward as if pulled by a giant magnet. You lose consciousness. When you awake, you are in a well-lighted and comfortable room. Three people are standing close to you. They look normal and appear to be friendly.

The middle one speaks. "You are in the nether region of Atlantis. This is a visitors' reception room. If you wish to come into the city of Atlantis, then follow us; but you may never return to your world. If you wish to leave now, we will escort you safely to the surface. It is your choice. We do not wish to harm you."

If you follow them into the city of Atlantis, turn to page 55.

If you decide to return to the surface, turn to page 51.

You are led to a room. The floors are a rich marble. The walls glow. The ceiling is like being inside a diamond looking through the many facets.

A person who immediately commands respect beckons you with firmness and kindness to come to her.

"Welcome to Atlantis. Thousands of years ago we learned that we were about to slip into the sea. Our people prepared for the calamity by building a new city inside an extinct volcano. We have lived here in peace and harmony ever since. We have no sunlight, nor stars to gaze at, but we have other spaces to meditate upon."

She tells you about a group of people called the Nodoors. If you wish, you can live with them, but you cannot leave Atlantis.

A bearded man is to be your escort. Atlantis is a beautiful city. Buildings merge one into another, colors radiate light, and coral branches fill courtyards. There is a sense of well-being and peace.

It would be pleasant here, but you don't want to be a prisoner. Maybe there would be a better chance to escape if you join the Nodoors. You ask your guide about them.

"Oh, we believe they are dangerous, but we don't really know. They live in the center of the old volcano. If you wish, I can take you there."

If you decide to join the Nodoors, turn to page 56.

If you decide to remain with the Atlanteans and perhaps get a chance to escape, turn to page 57.

The Atlanteans have lived in peace for thousands of years. They have no love of warfare. Their civilization is technologically very advanced and a sensing mechanism tells them that you are about to use your laser cannon. They quickly fire a special beam at the *Seeker* that makes all its functions stop. You are now powerless to escape. They walk up calmly to the *Seeker* and tell you to come with them to Atlantis.

"You are now part of Atlantis. We understand your fear, but do not be frightened. No harm will come to you and your life will be full. Follow us."

As you walk with them, into a new world, you wonder if you will *ever* see the sky again.

The End

You are greeted by a group of people who look like ordinary human beings except that there are gill-like slits on their necks. Their bare feet have skin between the toes forming a web. They order you to put on your sea suit, pull you quickly from the *Seeker*, and lead you towards their city. On the way they show you the zoo where there are animals from the world above the sea. There is a glass-like cage surrounding them filled with air, allowing them to live below the sea.

The leader of the group explains that if you wish you may either submit to an operation to have gills inserted so that you may breathe underwater, or you may join the other animals in the zoo.

If you agree to the operation, turn to page 58.

If you go to the zoo, turn to page 59.

Back aboard the *Seeker,* you radio the *Maray* that you are surfacing to make a plan. While rising out of the giant crevice-like canyon, you spot what appears to be a road running along the top of the ledge. What is this? The scientists aboard the *Maray* had mentioned the possibilities of finding signs of the ancient civilization, such as roads. You must investigate.

Turn to page 6.

You escape being seen by the submarine craft. Following the instructions you enter a passageway. At the end of the passageway is an airlock door and beyond it an incredibly large air-filled cavern. Perhaps it is the inside of an extinct volcano.

The land is pleasant, although strange to your experience. A soft substance covers the ground. It seems to be alive. You can't tell. A gentle light comes from the sides of this huge cavern. It reminds you of early morning light just before the sun rises.

A group of people approach you with friendly gestures. They are wearing simple clothes much like the clothes people wore in ancient Greece. They are kind and generous. You remove your diving suit to find that the air is good to breathe.

These people speak a language that is unknown to you, but one of them acts as an interpreter. You find out that this is Atlantis. They tell you it is governed by a man who is greedy, selfish, and dangerous. The people are like slaves. Everyone is unhappy except a few who serve the ruler as his lieutenants. These new friends ask for your help. Perhaps you can help them escape.

If you decide to leave your new friends and search for the ruler, turn to page 60.

If you decide to help your new friends escape, turn to page 61.

Quickly you get into the *Seeker* in an attempt to escape the strange submarine. You notice that the sub is chasing you so you put on full emergency ascent power. You could use your laser cannon to blast the sub, but you do not wish to hurt anyone.

The ascent towards the surface is swift, but a few fathoms from the surface all systems on the *Seeker* fail. You are suspended in the water in a helpless position. It seems that a mysterious force has disabled you.

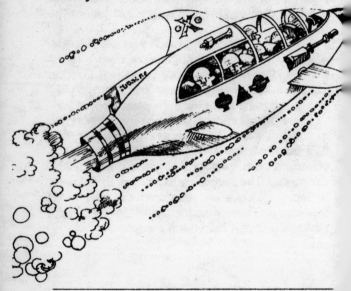

If you decide to wait on board the Seeker *for help from the Maray, turn to page 64.*

If you try to escape from the Seeker *and try for the surface on your own, turn to page 63.*

Cautiously you enter the ship's cabin. Clay jugs called amphorae, once filled with oils and wines, are strewn about. There are no remains of the crew. You do have a sense of being in ancient Greece and it is a strange feeling.

A door leads to a smaller cabin. On a table near the rear of this cabin is a golden box. You open it and find the remains of a map. It does not show Atlantis. It shows that the ship was searching for a hole that leads to the center of the earth!

You return to the *Seeker* and use the map to locate this incredible shaft to the center of the earth. Using some guesswork to interpret the map, you discover the tunnel opening, which appears to be roughly 100 feet in diameter. The sonar readings indicate the hole has no bottom.

If you decide to descend into the hole, turn to page 65.

If you decide it is time to go back up to the surface, turn to page 66.

The trip back to the surface is smooth, and finally the *Seeker* is hauled aboard the *Maray*. You climb out and are greeted by the scientists and crew. The *Seeker* is prepared for the second dive, but suddenly the wind rises and the sea kicks up into furious waves that crash over the deck of the *Maray*. All hands rush to prepare for hurricane force winds. There is no chance for the second dive to begin. All day and all night the *Maray* pitches on the stormy sea.

The next morning the wind has died and the sky is clear. You are now ready to dive again.

Turn to page 48.

A helicopter is sent to pick you up and return you to an air base for a flight back to the United States. Newspaper reports indicate that the search for Atlantis has been given up. Several months later, however, a group of scientists get in touch with you because they believe that Atlantis can be found. They have put together another expedition and want you to join it. You are tempted. Adventure into the unknown is what you like.

The End

Again the *Seeker* is lowered over the side of the *Maray* and slips into the ocean. Fish swim by peering cautiously at you in your metal shell. The sunlight fades as you descend into the abyss.

You are headed for the giant canyon below that might lead to Atlantis. When you reach the canyon you switch on the *Seeker's* searchlight. Immediately you spot the round hole that appears to be made by intelligent beings. Perhaps it leads to Atlantis.

Turn to page 9.

50

You are dizzy from lack of oxygen and fatigue. With your knife you slash away at the heavy brown kelp that surrounds you. Bit by bit, you seem to be getting free. Then suddenly you shoot up through the last clinging pieces of seaweed and reach the surface. You fire the special signal flare and the crew of the *Maray* quickly spots you. Within a few moments you are safely aboard, surrounded by your friends. What a relief to be out of that nightmare world!

If you dive again the next day,
turn to page 67.

If you want to rest a few days and
make emergency plans, turn to page 68.

The three people of Atlantis sense your wish to return to the surface. Instantly, they produce a bubble-shaped capsule and put you inside.

"Farewell, earth person. May you live a long and prosperous life."

You shoot up swiftly through the sea and break out onto the surface near the *Maray*. The capsule that protected you disintegrates upon reaching the surface. Once aboard the *Maray*, you tell the crew and the scientists about your adventure. They are kind to you, but no one believes you. They think you have imagined the world of Atlantis as a result of being so deep for so long.

Back in the United States, you begin a television tour telling about Atlantis. You write articles and a book. You are paid a great deal of money for this work. You are tempted to use this money for another expedition.

If you use your money for another expedition, turn to page 72.

If you decide to retire and lead a life of ease, turn to page 74.

The worst thing you could do would be to panic. You relax and drift with the current which suddenly takes you upward. With your knife, you cut through the kelp and are free. What a relief.

But no sooner do you get out of the kelp, than you are caught in the vortex of a giant whirlpool!

If you try to swim out of the whirlpool, turn to page 69.

If you dive into the vortex of the whirlpool hoping to reach the bottom and get out, turn to page 70.

The three people lead you into an enormous cavern. In the center of the cavern is a huge, silver-colored machine. It is shaped like a long tube with several round panels attached to one end.

They lead you inside. It is the most advanced control room that you have ever seen. Computers, sensing devices, recording devices, monitors, and a host of dials and panels fill the room. A strangely shaped figure with a very large head and totally blank eyes faces you.

"So, now you are in the control room of Atlantis. You see our secret. We landed on this planet 3000 years ago. We used our anti-matter device to sink this continent beneath the sea so we could escape from your people. You can have a most pleasant and useful life here with us if you wish. All you need to do is allow us to inject you with a special serum to enable you to live down here. It is up to you. On the other hand, if you do not wish to be one of us, you will be held prisoner."

*If you submit to the injection,
turn to page 71.*

If you decline, turn to page 73.

"I wish to join the Nodoors," you tell your guide. He leads you to the outskirts of the city.

"I must leave you now. Good luck." The Nodoors send a greeting party that is heavily armed. They are suspicious of you and believe that you are a spy sent by the Atlanteans. They look exactly like the Atlanteans, but they rarely smile.

"Come with us. You must be questioned. Perhaps you will work for us."

For 3 days you are questioned and kept in a small room without windows. These people are not kind and you believe that you have made a mistake. They ask you to help them spy on the Atlanteans. They suggest that, as a spy, you could pass freely between both groups.

If you decide to escape, turn to page 75.

If you decide to accept their offer, turn to page 76.

You decide to remain with the Atlanteans. Their approach to life seems ideal. Time is spent in creating things to help life and not to destroy it. You believe their leader is speaking the truth when she tells of avoiding war and of not hating.

You are fascinated by this apparently ideal world. You would like to stay and search out the history of how Atlantis became what it is and what caused the split between the Atlanteans and the Nodoors. Yet, in your mind remains the hope of escape so that you can go back to your own world.

If you decide to stay and spend your life searching out the history and secrets of Atlantis, turn to page 77.

If you decide to escape, turn to page 79.

A large white light shines down on you as you lie on the operating table. Then you become unconscious. Pleasant thoughts, sounds, and pictures occupy your mind. When you awake, you feel no pain nor any real change. But, now you can breathe underwater and join the Atlanteans in their world.

For several weeks you explore the world under the sea as you never have seen it before. Without the heavy oxygen equipment on your back, you feel a marvelous sense of energy and you glide through a world of beauty. Your two guides have become very good friends and they take you on adventures in the deep, exploring the ocean bottom and getting to know the fish and other sea creatures. It is a very exciting life indeed. You like it, but you regret that you will never again know the world above the sea.

The End

"No, I refuse to have this insane operation. I don't want to become a fish!"

The Atlanteans try to convince you that life with them will be happy, useful, and long. Yet, you still refuse. Sadly they give up their arguments and spray you with a special mist that immediately knocks you out. Several hours later you gain your senses only to find that you are in an underwater air tank where you breathe naturally. Your closest neighbor is a horse who looks at you with sorrow and understanding. The Atlanteans have built a small apartment very much like the ones in the world above the sea. People come by and look at you and talk with you.

Maybe you have made a real mistake. They no longer want you to join them in their world and way of life. You refused their offer and now you are a prisoner in a zoo.

The End

It doesn't take you long to find the king. One of his countless agents leads you to him. He is in a small simple room with a strange light glowing from the rounded ceiling.

"So, you have found your way here after all. Put your mind at rest. I won't hurt you." The king's booming voice startles you. He invites you to sit down.

After several hours with the king, you find him to be bright, friendly, and interesting. Maybe the Atlanteans are wrong about this person.

He offers you a chance to join his government. He tells you that most people are lazy and selfish and deserve to be ruled with power and command. He has been king for almost 1000 years and he has survived because he is not afraid to be tough. He wants you to be an advisor on his staff.

If you decide to accept the king's offer and work for him, turn to page 80.

If you decide to refuse and go back to join the other people, turn to page 82.

The problem is where do they escape to? The king is in charge. He rules the world below the sea and his spies are everywhere. The only answer is to devise a plan to capture the king and put him in prison.

The people are frightened. Some citizens tried to revolt years before and are still in prison. The king is smart and suspicious of everyone.

You suggest a plan to put on a festival with a play. On a given signal the actors and the people in the audience will rise up and seize the king. The actors will be carrying real weapons, but no one will suspect them because they are in the play.

The people like the plan. They ask you to become their leader.

If you accept their wish to become their leader, turn to page 81.

If you decide to help them in the planning, but also to escape from this sad world, turn to page 86.

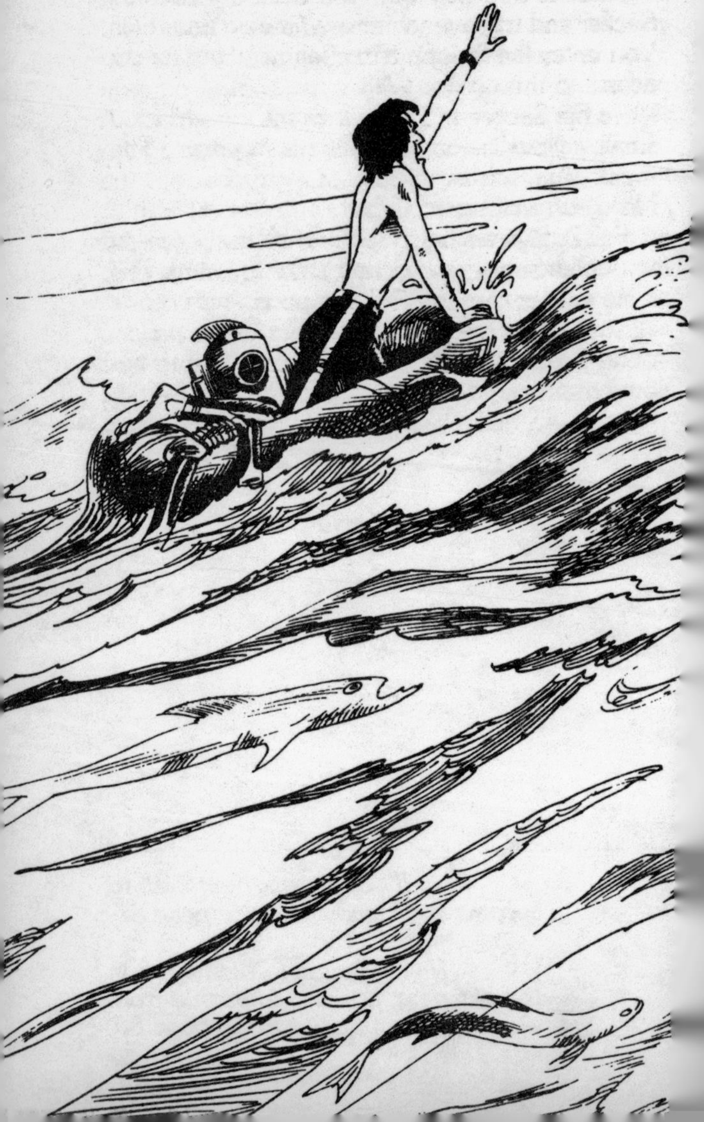

There is one way out, you decide. Leave the *Seeker* and try to reach the surface on your own. You enter the airlock chamber which gives you access to the ocean. With a quick push off, you leave the *Seeker* and swim towards the surface. A small, yellow life raft is part of your escape equipment. The surface of the sea is calm, but the *Maray* is nowhere in sight.

For 2 days and nights you drift in the life raft under hot sun and sharp starlight. At last a search helicopter spots you. Finally you are safe.

The exploration of Atlantis will have to depend on a new diver. Your eyesight has been damaged by the strange force that immobilized the *Seeker*. Your career as an underwater adventurer is over.

The End

The best plan is to wait until the *Maray* locates you with sonar equipment. You can't signal the ship because none of the *Seeker's* electronic equipment is working. There is no sign of the mysterious submarine. Perhaps it has left, now that you have been chased away from the world of Atlantis.

Looking out of the thick glass porthole, you see a giant blue whale heading for you. It looks as though the whale is going to ram you. Maybe the other submarine has angered the whale and it is seeking revenge on any craft near it.

Suddenly the whale hits you full force. The *Seeker* is badly damaged. Water begins to trickle in through the hatch cover. You must abandon the *Seeker*. The whale now remains close to the *Seeker* watching and waiting.

*If you decide to try and escape,
turn to page 63.*

*If you try to hitch a ride on the whale,
turn to page 85.*

*If you don't know what to do,
turn to page 87.*

Why not go? Who would believe it? The center of the earth! You push the control column forward and dive deep. Soon there is no more water, just a heavy gas that acts like water. You look at a world of colors and drifting forms. You pass by layers of rock and sand. Suddenly you sail into a gooey mass which almost fouls the *Seeker's* propellers. Then the *Seeker's* engine stops and you are pulled along through the semi-liquid material by something like gravity or magnetism. You burst through a thick elastic membrane and enter an area of giant atoms. Electrons whirl around you at high speed, but there is plenty of room to maneuver between these fast-moving particles. The electrons are revolving around a small mass you know is called the nucleus. You are able to avoid collisions with the electrons. What a world! Maybe you are having hallucinations.

If you continue on in this trip to the center of the earth, turn to page 88.

If you try to turn back, turn to page 89.

You face the fact that it is too dangerous to dive into a deep hole that might lead to the center of the earth. It is better judgment to return to the surface and work out a plan of action.

You give one last look at the opening, check the *Seeker's* instruments and head up to the surface. Finally the *Seeker* breaks through into fresh air and sunlight and you wait to be picked up by the *Maray*.

Turn to page 32.

You insist that you are all right and will dive again the next day. The scientists try to convince you that it is foolhardy to go down again so soon. The captain of the *Maray* reports that a large storm system is coming and the next day will probably be the last day of diving for some time.

Against advice, you enter the *Seeker,* wave farewell to all your friends and descend into the deep. You feel tired but excited.

When you reach the bottom, you decide to explore the ledge along the deep canyon.

Turn to page 6.

A violent storm is reported heading your way. The captain decides to move the *Maray* to the shelter of a nearby island harbor. It is too dangerous to remain where you are. Deckhands lash the *Seeker* securely to the deck of the *Maray* and you get underway.

The storm breaks before you can reach the island harbor. The *Seeker* is torn loose and lost overboard. The monitors aboard the *Maray* are damaged by a frightful electric storm discharge. You are all alive but there are no funds to replace the damaged equipment. The expedition to Atlantis is over.

The End

It is no use. The whirlpool has you in its grip.
You feel your arms and legs being torn in every
direction. There is no way out. Round and round
you go.

*If you use your laser pistol to
blast a hole in the whirlpool wall,
turn to page 97.*

*If you continue to struggle,
turn to page 98.*

You decide that you can't swim out of the whirlpool. There is only one thing to do. Dive deep into the center.

You kick several times and hurl yourself into the center of the whirlpool. Lights and colors dance before your eyes. You lose all track of where you are. You find yourself standing on the ocean floor. You can look up through the center of the whirlpool and see the sky more than 2000 feet above you. It is a tiny patch of blue.

If you try to return to the surface, turn to page 99.

If you set out to explore this strange area, turn to page 100.

Perhaps you are being foolish, but you decide to join them. The injection is painless and you feel no different than before. They lead you to a comfortable room where you all share a special tea in celebration of your decision.

"You see, all living beings are basically the same. Everything is connected in life. We have come from a different planet in search of other living beings. We have to be very careful about taking new people to our planet. Some of your people seek us out, just like you. We choose carefully."

You are amazed at what they say. A choice is given to you. You can either journey with them through time and space to their planet, or you can remain in underwater Atlantis as a worker recording information about life on earth.

If you decide to travel with them in space and time, turn to page 90.

If you decide to stay in Atlantis as a worker, turn to page 91.

The only way to prove that you are not crazy is to lead another expedition back to Atlantis. You take all the money from the TV appearances and articles and outfit a boat, hire a crew, rent the *Seeker,* and set sail. Most people think that you are out of your mind. You will show them.

Poised over the spot you so carefully marked on the charts, you dive down in the *Seeker.* Again you find the hidden grotto and the round metal panel.

The panel seems to seal off a passageway. It is locked. You try to open it with the *Seeker's* drilling arm, but it will not budge. It is frustrating to be so close to the secret and yet so far from it.

Should you blast the panel with the laser beam? If so, turn to page 93.

If you wait patiently to be observed and asked in, turn to page 94.

The idea of being injected with a serum and joining them for the rest of your life is awful. You must plan an escape.

When your captors are not looking, you slip away and dash for the door of the space craft. You fail to notice a laser beam guarding the exit hatch. Stepping into the laser beam, you freeze in mid-step. The Atlanteans gather round you sadly and tell you that you will have to remain this way for the earth equivalent of 23 years and 61 days until the effects wear off. Then you will be given a second chance.

The End

You argue with yourself for several weeks about setting out on a new expedition. Money is not the issue. You fear that finding Atlantis will ruin it for the Atlanteans. You believe that their civilization must be protected. You decide to use the money you have made to carry on research on space and life on planets in other galaxies. Someday perhaps you will meet the Atlanteans in space.

The End

*If you don't like this ending,
turn to page 107.*

Escape will be difficult, but you decide that you must get away from these people. The best plan is to tell them that you want to accept their offer to spy on the Atlanteans. They are of course happy when you tell them that you will work for them.

"You see, the Atlanteans are jealous of us. We must be on our guard or else they will invade our area and capture us."

You don't believe the Atlanteans are at all jealous of the Nodoors, but you won't argue. They take you back to the outskirts of their area, and you leave to join the Atlanteans. Once back with the Atlanteans, you ask them to allow you to live with them. You know that you will never be allowed to leave their underwater world, but there is always the hope for escape. It could be a good life.

The End

"Ok, I'll do it," you say. "I'll join you and spy on the Atlanteans for you. Who knows, maybe they aren't as bad as you think."

The Nodoors are delighted that you will help them. They give you a room in a large building where most of them live. It is grey and forbidding, more like a prison than anything else. That night when all are asleep, you sit sleepless and realize that you are caught in a trap of your own making. It comes to you that the Nodoors are from a different planet and are unhappy outcasts. The Atlanteans want nothing to do with them. You chose the wrong side.

The End

If you don't like this ending, turn to page 108.

Maybe you can learn from the Atlanteans how they achieve such happiness in their lives. You will seek out their history.

When you announce your decision to stay, you are treated with kindness and friendship. You explain that you would like to help in their underwater food production.

Atlantis was an advanced civilization thousands of years ago. The citizens nourished their peaceful thoughts and plucked out their hateful thoughts as one would tend a garden. Their minds became a rich and dazzling universe, clear and unbounded.

You have so much to do, helping with sea plants and studying their history that you soon forget the *Seeker*.

The End

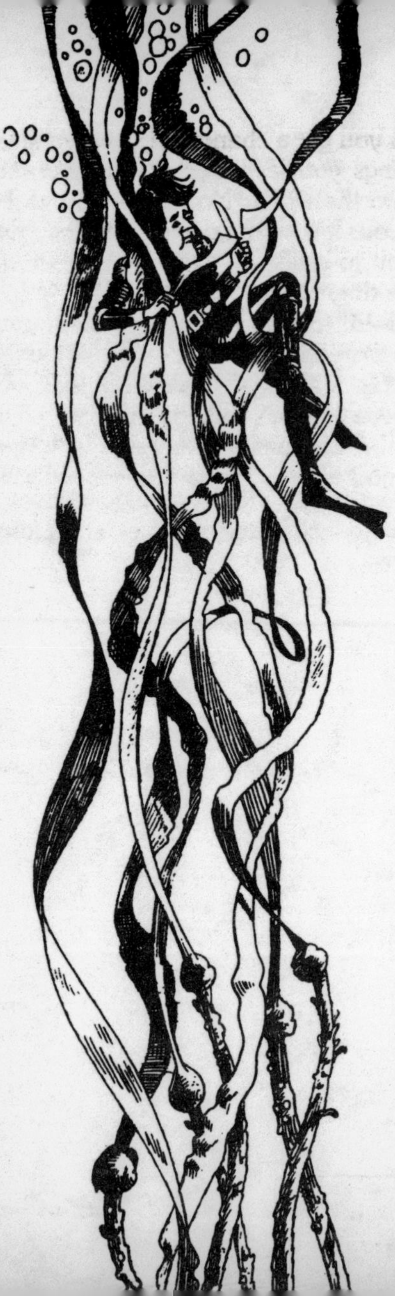

When you get a chance and everyone is doing other things, you dash for the tunnel exit and make it out into the water. No alarms sound. No one chases you. It is strange; they said they wouldn't allow you to return to the world above the sea. Why are they letting you escape?

You swim toward the surface; then you black out. It is too deep. No one could survive the pressure and lack of oxygen. But a miracle has happened because you suddenly find yourself hacking away at brown seaweed that surrounds you and you are just a short way from the surface.

Turn to page 50.

An advisor to a king! What a chance. Maybe the king has ruled so long that he is out of touch with the people. Perhaps as his advisor you can help the people get what they want. You don't believe that people are lazy and selfish. The king just needs a new point of view.

You are appointed the king's special advisor on problems of research on food and shelter. You immediately call general meetings of all the people to discuss the food program and the work schedules. The king is so glad to have someone else take over the problems that he leaves it in your hands entirely. He gives you land and a large salary. You set up new programs and schedules. The people are involved in the planning and the work. You listen to their complaints and their ideas. Life under the sea is rich and full. The people are hard working and good. It was a wise decision to remain.

The End

You do not wish to lead a revolt but the people need you. You organize the play, and the king is pleased to have his people involved in a project that keeps them busy and happy. The people can't wait for the day when they can put the king in prison and make their own decisions.

The night of the play, the theater is filled, and everyone waits for the king to appear. But there is a delay. The crowd grows nervous. Then a messenger from the king runs into the theater and announces that the king has had a serious attack of brain fever. He may not live.

You wonder whether the king is really ill or whether he has found out about the plot against him. The people are confused and do not know what to do. They turn to you and you tell them to go on with the play. Just then, a squad of the king's soldiers enters the theater. They are headed for you.

If you allow them to capture you, turn to page 116.

If you try to escape, turn to page 117.

Advisor to a mean king? Not a chance! You tell him that you want nothing to do with a tyrant who doesn't believe in people. You tell him to his face that the people are unhappy and angry. He laughs and tells you to go back to them if you wish. He warns you that the people are complainers, not workers.

Once back with your new friends, you discuss how to overthrow the king and his henchmen. You hold secret meetings and work out a plan. But on the day of the overthrow, someone discovers a leak in the volcano wall of the underwater world. The entire civilization is in danger. All thoughts of revolt are forgotten. The Atlanteans must stop the sea from crashing in on them. Everyone works for a common purpose. Survival is the goal.

If you decide to work with them in this time of disaster, turn to page 112.

If you decide to take advantage of this emergency to escape, turn to page 114.

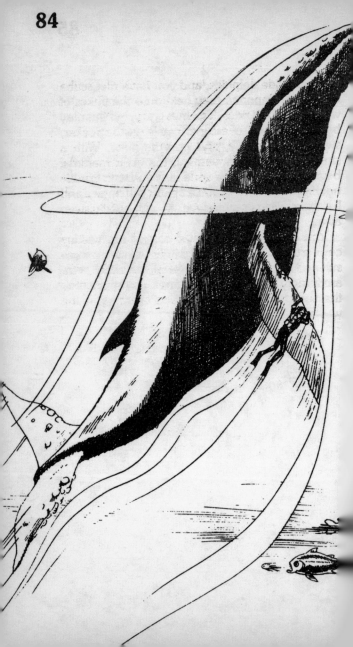

People ride dolphins, and you have met scuba divers who reported they held onto the flukes of whales for short rides. It sounds crazy, but this may be your only way of escape. You leave the *Seeker*, swim to the whale, and grab its fluke. With a smooth powerful movement, the giant mammal begins to swim to the surface. You have trouble holding on. Then the whale breaks the surface and lies there filling its lungs with air. You quietly swim away.

You drift for 2 or 3 days, dozing and waking comfortably. You stay warm in your insulated sea suit and its special air packs keep you afloat. You are hungry and thirsty, but unharmed by the time the search helicopter spots you bobbing in the waves.

The End

It is their world, but you are willing to help them with the planning for the overthrow of the king. You want no real part in the revolt.

The planning requires choosing new leaders and setting goals for the people. You almost decide to join them in the actual revolt, but you really want to get back to your own world. Once the revolt is underway, you hope to slip away and return to the *Seeker* for a quick escape to the surface of the ocean.

The day of the revolt, you can't resist the excitement of the Atlanteans' bold enterprise, and you decide to stay with them and help in any way that you can. The endless planning and training pays off. The carefully selected band of men and women easily capture the king and his guards. The revolt has succeeded without shedding a drop of blood and the people celebrate for days.

The Atlanteans treat you as if you are one of them, and, for the first time, you feel that you are.

The End

You admit that you just don't know what to do. The whale is frightening looking and you don't have any escape plans. So you wait and watch and listen.

After what seems a long time, but is probably just a few minutes, the mysterious submarine returns, attaches a cable to the *Seeker*, and pulls you up to the surface. Then the submarine vanishes under the waves, leaving you to wait for the *Maray*.

The End

The electrons whirl about at dizzy speeds and you continue until you get to a spot where your instruments indicate that there is no time. The clocks stop, the speed indicator stops, your heart stops, and yet you are alive. Every sense in your body seems more alive than ever before. You hear beautiful music and see lights that you feel and taste as well. Peace and well-being fill you.

You become aware of other beings close to you. No one has entered through the only hatch and yet there are other presences in the *Seeker*. Turning around, you see three Atlanteans. Then you feel that the *Seeker* has become just a thought and that the people from Atlantis have entered your mind and are aboard the *Seeker*. You try to enter their thoughts, but they tell you that you have not journeyed far enough yet to be able to become a thought traveler.

If you try to turn back from this strange world, turn to page 95.

If you decide to travel in thought-time-space, turn to page 96.

No, you will not dive down toward the center of the earth. Once through the thin outer layer of the earth, you know that the regions beneath change from solid to molten and then to a hard core. At least that is the theory given by the scientists. You couldn't possibly survive such a journey. Anyway, you think that your sonar gear is probably not working correctly. The hole is deep, but you don't believe that it really goes all the way to the center of the earth. Caution is your approach. You go back to the surface to consult with the scientists aboard the *Maray*.

The scientists tell you that their instruments have been damaged, perhaps by an approaching storm, and they too, are cautious. They decide to move the *Maray* away from the site of the mysterious hole. The expedition retreats and you know your chance to discover Atlantis has slipped away.

The End

"I will go with you. I want to see other parts of the universe."

"Congratulations. You will not regret this. We are ready to depart."

They take you to a small room and three of them stand with you under a beam of intense light. You feel a rush of speed, and yet you are not moving. You feel as though you have traveled hundreds of thousands of miles in space. You rush past the sun, past and through the Milky Way, and on into other galaxies. Yet, you feel as though you are still standing in the same spot.

Then you are on the planet Aygr where the Atlanteans came from. It is a world of fantastic shapes and strange plants. The city gleams like a thousand search lights. The shapes that must be their buildings are pure light pulsing with energy. Nothing is hard or sharp. Everything is light. You see no people, just forms of brighter light that move. Suddenly, some of the moving forms change into Atlanteans.

"Our bodies are not important. It is our energy that is important. You can see us in our body forms if you wish, but we only use them to communicate with people like you. You may choose to remain as you are or accept transformation."

If you decide to stay in your body form, turn to page 101.

If you decide to be transformed into an energy shape, turn to page 102.

You have had enough adventure for now. Travel to another planet in a different galaxy sounds like more risk than you wish to take. Besides, you can always go later.

You tell the people that you wish to stay and work in their society. Perhaps your knowledge of the sea can help them. They discuss your case very seriously for several days. When they are through talking, they offer you a choice of jobs in Atlantis. You may become a farmer or a musician.

If you decide to become an underwater farmer, turn to page 103.

If you decide to become a musician, turn to page 104.

You'll try to blast the hatch right off its hinges. You have the power. Your finger presses the red button that fires the laser cannon. A blinding flash erupts immediately. But the hatch remains firm. You fire again and again and again. Each time the *Seeker* is rocked by the force of the laser cannon. The reflected energy is damaging to your craft. You continue to fire the cannon, holding your finger on the button.

Then there is a blinding flash inside the *Seeker* itself. The laser cannon has exploded. You and the *Seeker* are destroyed instantly. The hatch remains closed.

The End

It is never good to use force unless you are attacked and must defend yourself. You refuse even to consider using the laser cannon; it might kill people and would certainly destroy any chance for friendship. You decide to wait patiently and hope that you will be noticed and invited in.

For six hours you sit quietly and wait for some sign. A green glow comes from the area ahead of you. It bathes the *Seeker* in a gentle light. The hatch door opens. Three figures emerge and beckon to you to follow them.

If you follow, turn to page 105.

If you refuse to follow them turn to page 106

This is too much for you. It is like a nightmare and you decide to turn back. But going back is much harder than you expected. The electrons whirl closer and closer to you as though they were guards keeping you from leaving. It is difficult to guide the *Seeker* in this maze of atoms. The instruments are useless now. The figures of the Atlanteans disappear. Suddenly, you are caught in the elastic membrane that almost stopped you before. It sticks to the *Seeker,* holding you back. You want to be free and return to the world you have known all your life.

You lose consciousness and wake up several hours later in your sea suit floating above the hole in the ocean floor. The *Seeker* is gone. You're dazed: did you dream the whole thing? Slowly you return to the surface, but the *Maray* has disappeared. You can't decide how much time has elapsed. You realize that your crew must think you are lost forever and you know they are right. The waves rock your unresisting body back and forth as you float alone in the vast sea. You feel your strength slowly draining away.

The End

A thought traveler! You realize that people do it all the time in day dreams. Of course, you want to be a thought traveler, but how?

The Atlanteans speak softly and tell you that all things are the same—past, present, future are all the same. It simply requires you to concentrate and put your thoughts where you wish them to be.

You try, and amazingly you are rapidly rushed through time to the day you were born, then to the day you made your first deep-sea dive. Your mind flies from one time in your life to another. But when it comes to the future, you meet a blank wall. You can't seem to travel into the future.

"Why can't I travel ahead in time," you ask the Atlanteans.

"Be patient," they reply. "All in good time."

Suddenly you whirl through time into the outer reaches of the universe where you can actually feel the light going through you. You cast no shadow. A sense of peace fills you.

If you decide to drop out of thought travel and return to earth life, turn to page 110.

If not, turn to page 111.

You have a laser pistol that you carry for emergencies. You blast a hole in the whirlpool wall and dive through it. Facing you is a school of fish who are puzzled by this strange intruder. Behind them lurks the form of a shark. You swim toward the surface slowly and the shark vanishes into the deep.

The *Maray* is nowhere in sight. You are wondering how long you'll be waiting when a loud splashing sighing sound startles you. A huge whale has surfaced and lies nearby spouting and sucking in great noisy draughts of air. It take you a good half hour to swim to the enormous creature. It pays no attention to you. You climb onto its tail and crawl on hands and knees toward the highest point of its back. It's like creeping up a gigantic grey rock.

From your vantage point on top, sure enough, you can see the *Maray* and the tiny glint of binocular lenses reflecting in the sun. The *Maray* crew is watching the whale. You wave, feeling certain they have seen you. It won't be long before they come to collect you.

The End

You faint, and when you come to, you are floating on the surface of the ocean. There is a heavy ocean swell and the sun beats down on you. The whirlpool must have stopped as quickly and mysteriously as it began. You feel dizzy and exhausted and you move gently to make sure you haven't broken any bones. As you move your head slowly inside your helmet, you feel an intense pain shooting across your right temple. You have to lie very still then and gradually your ears pick up the thrum of the search helicopter. You don't dare move to look, but as the minutes go by, the thrum gets louder and slowly disappears. The helicopter has passed over you. It won't return this way. The pain in your temple increases. You begin to lose consciousness.

The End

The walls of the whirlpool look like solid ridges sloping upwards to the surface. The water is rushing so fast that the center looks absolutely calm. You wonder if perhaps you could swim up through that calm. It's worth a try, and you set off. Before you can tell if you're making any progress, the whirlpool reverses and instead of whirling down, it whirls up and catapults you out of the ocean and into the air. You fall back onto the surface of the ocean close to the *Maray*. Although you are stunned by the fall, you quickly gain your senses and are picked up by the ship. Of course no one believes your story, but then even you think it is almost too fantastic to have happened.

The End

100

The ocean floor has a small metal hatch on it. You pull with all your strength but it will not open. You rest for a moment and look through the wall of water surrounding you. Two fish stare back at you! It's as though you are in an aquarium for the fish to look at.

You don't hear the hatch open. A voice commands you to enter. With fear and caution you walk down a corridor that leads to a small room. Three people meet you.

Turn to page 55

You just can't give up your body. It might be all right for the Atlanteans to move about as pure energy, but you have not reached a point where you are willing to risk what you are for what they are.

It is strange wandering about with bright glowing blobs of energy moving with you. They ask you to give talks about life on earth as you know it, and you agree. For two years you meet with the Atlanteans in their energy forms and talk about earth and how people live and what they do. The Atlanteans are interested in all aspects of earth life: the technology, politics, wars, and religion.

You ask them why, but they never give you a direct answer. Then one day you look down at yourself and you only see bright, glowing energy. With horror you realize you have become one of them.

The End

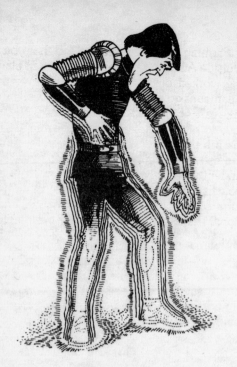

You are in the Atlantean world; why not become like an Atlantean? Looking down at your hands, you see them gradually begin to glow with a warm, yellow light. Little by little, the glow travels up your arms and legs until suddenly you have no body left. You are a glowing energy form. You feel a sense of freedom and happiness that you have never known before. You can float, or fly, or zoom anywhere you want to. No walls stop you; you just melt through them. You don't need food or rest. You can travel through time, and you can travel instantly back to earth in your energy form.

You feel that this is the way you want to be.

The End

Farming under the sea is a job that you enjoy. Outside Atlantis, there are fields of sea plants that are worked on just like gardens above the sea. Atlanteans go out each day and harvest the plants, take care of the fields, and chase away the fish that love to nibble on the growing plants. Then there are fish pens to work on. There you feed and tend the fish until they are needed for food. Farming under the sea is beautiful and it is much easier than you had imagined. Danger lurks, though, in the form of sting rays, slender sea snakes, and occasional sharks. You have to be on your guard at all times.

The End

A musician in the world of Atlantis. Who would believe it? You are asked to choose an instrument to play. You examine water lutes, sea drums, shark bone flutes, and a wide range of electronic instruments. You choose one of the electronic instruments, but it makes no sound at all. You are told that it plays music that people feel rather than hear. What a world you're living in! Who would believe in music that is not heard? Gradually you learn to feel the different notes with parts of your body: your thighs, chest, temples, and fingertips. Your interest in this new way of sensing music grows with each day. You master this new art form. You become their greatest musician.

The End

These people lead you to a control room. There you meet the commander of an underwater scientific center that is conducting secret research into life underneath the sea. They inform you that it was a good thing that you did not use your laser cannon, because they have anti-laser devices that would have blown you and the *Seeker* to pieces.

After a pleasant meal and a tour of the deep-water lab, you are sent back to the *Seeker* for a return journey to the surface. You are told never to return again; if you do, you will be kept a prisoner for the rest of your life.

The End

When you refuse to follow them, they take out small hand-held hypnotizers that put you into a deep trance. You are led through a long tunnel into a large underwater lab. Three military technicians come up to you and break the trance.

"You have stumbled into a secret military base. We're developing too many secret plans to risk being discovered. You will remain our prisoner."

There is no escape.

The End

You argue with yourself for weeks. Then you decide to go back to Atlantis. You are in such a hurry to return that you hire a small, fast hydrofoil craft to take you to the spot in the ocean where Atlantis is. Once reaching the spot, you intend to make a dive with just scuba gear! You know a 2000-foot dive is impossible. But you don't care; you feel you must make the attempt.

A storm rips the sea for six days and when it clears you prepare to dive. Just as you slip into the water, you look up into the sky and high above the clouds you see the sparkling city of Atlantis. No dive is necessary.

The End

During the night, you are awakened by the sound of voices talking quietly. Listening, you realize that a group of Nodoors is planning an escape. They want to join the Atlanteans. They believe that life in Atlantis can be better for them. You join them and listen to the stories of fear and darkness. They seek light and friendship. It sounds simple, but nothing is easy.

Suddenly the door bursts open. Three guards armed with special weapons rush in. They fire the weapons and in a flash of brilliant light you and your companions are vaporized.

The End

Over 1000 years of thought travel later, you are called into the main thinking room. You are told that you may now return to earth life. You have doubts about going back, but you are curious to see what changes have occurred while you were living in Atlantis.

What a sight greets you as you circle earth at an altitude of 1000 feet! The great cities of the world, New York, London, Paris, and Hong Kong are overgrown with vegetation. The roads leading into the cities are barely visible. But you see signs of new settlements. There are clusters of buildings spread out in the countryside. You don't see any smokestacks. There are few roads and no cars. The people live a simple life providing themselves with food, shelter, and clothing. You wish to join them.

The End

One day your friends tell you that you can return to earth if you wish. You consider it carefully and decide that because of your thought traveling ability, the life you now lead is what you want. You decide to stay where you are forever.

The End

Years ago the Atlanteans had worked out emergency procedures, but most people had forgotten them. One old person remembers where the emergency instructions and equipment were kept.

You and the Atlanteans work without stop for 72 hours pumping out the flooding waters and building a special retaining wall around the volcanic crack. Finally the last pump is shut off. You are all exhausted, but you've won in your battle against the sea.

The End

With everyone worried about the sea crashing in, no one will notice you if you try to escape. You run down a long, little-used corridor that leads to the sea. The exit door is heavy and rusty from not being used. You push with all your might, and finally it swings open into an airlock to the open water. You push the emergency release button and shoot out into the water. The *Seeker* is where you left it, and once inside, you head for the surface where the *Maray* waits for you.

The End

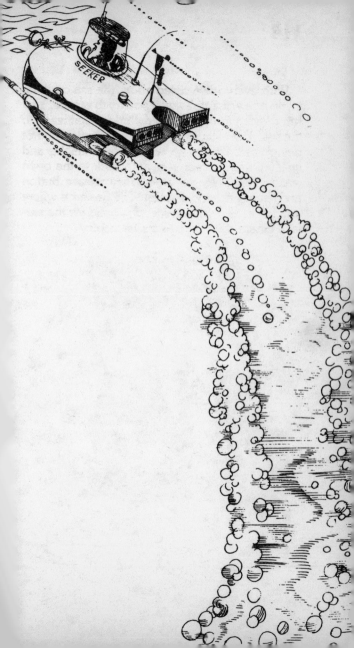

It is useless to try to escape the soldiers. You are surrounded. They take you to the king, and he sadly tells you that you are just like all the rest. He can't trust anyone. He will have to decide what to do with you and in the meantime he throws you into the dungeon.

The End

How can you escape? The soldiers are coming after you. You yell as loud as you can and everyone in the theater surrounds you, forming a barrier to the soldiers. The soldiers stare at the people all around them, hesitate, and then quickly leave. They know that the odds are too great to win such a fight.

The people cry for the revolt to go on. The crowd leaves the theater and heads to the king's quarters. All along the route people join you and even the king's soldiers begin to join the crowd. You and the people are free; the king is put in prison. The revolt is a success.

The End

ABOUT THE AUTHOR AND ILLUSTRATOR

R. A. Montgomery is an educator and the publisher of Vermont Crossroads Press, which he founded in 1974. He holds degrees from Williams College, the Divinity School at Yale University, and New York University (in Development Economics). After serving in a variety of administrative capacities at Williston Academy and Columbia University, he founded the Waitsfield Summer School in 1965, where he was headmaster for three years. Montgomery went on to found a research and development firm in 1968 and worked for several years as a consultant to the Peace Corps in Washington, D.C. and West Africa, responsible for training overseas staff.

A graduate of Pratt Institute, *Paul Granger* is a prize-winning illustrator and painter.

CHOOSE YOUR OWN ADVENTURE

☐	25763	PRISONER OF THE ANT PEOPLE #25	$2.25
☐	25916	THE PHANTOM SUBMARINE #26	$2.25
☐	26309	THE HORROR OF HIGH RIDGE #27	$2.25
☐	26252	MOUNTAIN SURVIVAL #28	$2.25
☐	26308	TROUBLE ON PLANET EARTH #29	$2.25
☐	26374	THE CURSE OF BATTSLEA HALL #30	$2.25
☐	26185	VAMPIRE EXPRESS #31	$2.25
☐	25764	TREASURE DIVER #32	$2.25
☐	25918	THE DRAGON'S DEN #33	$2.25
☐	24344	THE MYSTERY OF HIGHLAND CREST #34	$1.95
☐	25961	JOURNEY TO STONEHENGE #35	$2.25
☐	24522	THE SECRET TREASURE OF TIBET #36	$1.95
☐	25778	WAR WITH THE EVIL POWER MASTER #37	$2.25
☐	25818	SUPERCOMPUTER #39	$2.25
☐	26265	THE THRONE OF ZEUS #40	$2.25
☐	26062	SEARCH FOR MOUNTAIN GORILLAS #41	$2.25
☐	26313	THE MYSTERY OF ECHO LODGE #42	$2.25
☐	26522	GRAND CANYON ODYSSEY #43	$2.25
☐	24892	THE MYSTERY OF URA SENKE #44	$1.95
☐	26386	YOU ARE A SHARK #45	$2.25
☐	24991	THE DEADLY SHADOW #46	$1.95
☐	26388	OUTLAWS OF SHERWOOD FOREST #47	$2.25
☐	25134	SPY FOR GEORGE WASHINGTON #48	$1.95
☐	25177	DANGER AT ANCHOR MINE #49	$1.95
☐	25296	RETURN TO CAVE OF TIME #50	$1.95
☐	25242	MAGIC OF THE UNICORN #51	$2.25
☐	25488	GHOST HUNTER #52	$2.25
☐	25489	CASE OF THE SILK KING #53	$2.25
☐	25490	FOREST OF FEAR #54	$2.25
☐	25491	TRUMPET OF TERROR #55	$2.25
☐	25861	ENCHANTED KINGDOM #56	$2.25
☐	25741	THE ANTIMATTER FORMULA #57	$2.25
☐	25813	STATUE OF LIBERTY ADVENTURE #58	$2.25
☐	25885	TERROR ISLAND #59	$2.25
☐	25941	VANISHED! #60	$2.25
☐	26169	BEYOND ESCAPE! #61	$2.25

Prices and availability subject to change without notice.

Bantam Books, Inc., Dept. AV, 414 East Golf Road, Des Plaines, Ill. 60016

Please send me the books I have checked above. I am enclosing $_____
(please add $1.50 to cover postage and handling). Send check or money order
—no cash or C.O.D.s please.

Mr/Mrs/Miss _____

Address _____

City _____ State/Zip _____

AV—12/86

Please allow four to six weeks for delivery. This offer expires 5/87.

**BANTAM
SHOP·AT·HOME
C·A·T·A·L·O·G**

Shop at home
for quality childrens books
and save money, too.

Now you can order books for the whole family from
Bantam's latest listing of hundreds of titles includin
many fine children's books. *And* this special offer giv
you an opportunity to purchase a Bantam book f
only 50¢. Here's how:

By ordering any five books at the regular price p
order, you can also choose any other single book list
(up to $4.95 value) for just 50¢. Some restrictions
apply, so for further details send for Bantam's listi
of titles today.

BANTAM BOOKS, INC.
P.O. Box 1006, South Holland, ILL. 60473

Mr./Mrs./Miss/Ms. _____
(please print)

Address _____

City_____ State _____ Zip _____
FC(D)—11/8:

Printed in the U.S.A.